The Jewel Fairies

To Rachel and Anna Prockter,
two fairy friends

Special thanks to
Linda Chapman

ORCHARD BOOKS
338 Euston Road, London NW1 3BH
Orchard Books Australia
Hachette Children's Books
Level 17/207 Kent Street, Sydney, NSW 2000
A Paperback Original
First published in Great Britain in 2005
Rainbow Magic is a registered trademark of Working Partners Limited.
Series created by Working Partners Limited, London W6 OQT
Text © Working Partners Limited 2005
Illustrations © Georgie Ripper 2005
The right of Georgie Ripper to be identified as the illustrator
of this work has been asserted by her in accordance
with the Copyright, Designs and Patents Act, 1988.
A CIP catalogue record for this book is available
from the British Library.
ISBN 1 84362 956 9
7 9 10 8
Printed in Great Britain

Chloe
the Topaz
Fairy

by Daisy Meadows

illustrated by Georgie Ripper

ORCHARD BOOKS

www.rainbowmagic.co.uk

The
Fairyland
Palace

Adventure
Playground

Tippington
Manor

Tippington
Town

The Tall
Toy
Store

Fountain

Twisty Tree

Jack Frost's Ice Castle

Pegasus

Cherrywell Village

FANCY DRESS

Rachel's House

Buttercup Farm

Scarecrow

Chestnut Tree

By Frosty magic I cast away
These seven jewels with their fiery rays,
So their magic powers will not be felt
And my icy castle shall not melt.

The fairies may search high and low
To find the gems and take them home.
But I will send my goblin guards
To make the fairies' mission hard.

Contents

Goblins in Disguise!

"There's a fancy dress shop!"
Kirsty Tate said, pointing at one
of the shops on Cherrywell's busy
high street.

"Brilliant!" Rachel Walker replied
happily. "Let's go and choose
costumes for Isabel's Halloween
party before the bus arrives."

"OK," Kirsty agreed. She was staying at Rachel's house for half-term week and the girls had just been bowling with some of Rachel's friends from school. One of them, Isabel, had invited everyone to a Halloween party at the weekend. "What do you want to dress up as?" Kirsty asked Rachel.

"Something magical, of course!" Rachel replied with a grin.

Kirsty smiled back. She and Rachel loved magic.

It was because they shared an amazing secret: they were friends with the fairies!

Their magical adventures had started one summer when the girls had helped the fairies stop Jack Frost from taking the colour away from Fairyland. Since then, the Fairy King and Queen had asked for their help several times. In fact, that very week, Rachel and Kirsty were right in the middle of another fairy adventure, because Jack Frost was causing trouble again!

This time he'd stolen seven sparkling jewels from Queen Titania's tiara. The jewels were very precious because they controlled special fairy powers, like the fairies' ability to fly, or to give children in the human world sweet dreams. Every year, in a special celebration, the fairies would recharge their wands with the jewels' magic. This year's ceremony was due to take place in just a few days' time.

If the gems weren't found by then, the
fairies would run out of the jewels'
special magic completely!

Jack Frost had hoped to keep the
magic jewels himself. But when their
magical light had started to melt his ice
castle, he had flown into a rage and
cast a spell to hurl the gems into the
human world. Then he sent his mean
goblin servants to guard them so that
the fairies couldn't get them back.

Rachel and Kirsty had already helped
three of the Jewel Fairies recover their
magic gems, but there were still four
jewels left to find.

"Do you think we'll find another
jewel today?" Rachel whispered as she
and Kirsty ran up to the shop.

"I hope so," Kirsty replied.

A small boy and his mum were looking at the display in the window of the fancy dress shop. There were bright orange Halloween banners, pumpkin lanterns and two shop dummies wearing children's Halloween costumes – one dressed as a witch and one as a goblin.

Suddenly the boy gasped. "Mum! Did you see that?" he cried. "The model in that goblin costume moved!"

Rachel and Kirsty stopped and stared at each other.

"Don't be silly, Tom," the boy's mum laughed, leading him away. "Come along."

"A goblin model that moved?" Kirsty hissed to Rachel. "We'd better have a look."

They peered closely at the window display. The dummy the boy had pointed out was wearing a green goblin costume and a little red pointed hat. But Rachel's eyes widened as she took in the goblin's beady eyes, long nose and great big feet.

"That's not a goblin costume!" she exclaimed. "It's a *real* goblin in a tunic and a hat!"

"And look at the witch," Kirsty added.
The witch model sported a long
black skirt, a pointed hat
and a broomstick, but its
lumpy green nose and
warty chin looked
distinctly goblin-like to her.

"The witch is a goblin,
too!" Rachel gasped.

A thought hit Kirsty and she clutched at
Rachel's arm in excitement. "Oh, Rachel,
if there are goblins in the window, maybe
one of the fairies' magic jewels is inside
the shop!"

Looking out for Magic

"Come on. Let's go and see!" Rachel urged.

Pushing the door open, the girls hurried down three stone steps into the shop. An assistant came bustling to meet them. She had curly brown hair and a cheerful face. "Hello," she said, stepping around a large pile of pumpkin lanterns near the door. "Can I help you?"

Rachel could feel her heart pounding. "Um…" she began uncertainly. It was hard to concentrate knowing that there were two goblins standing just a few feet away.

"Could we look at some costumes please?" Kirsty put in quickly. "We're going to a Halloween party at the weekend and we haven't got anything to wear."

The shop assistant smiled. "Well, you've come to the right place! My name's Maggie and I'm sure I can sort you both out with something. What did you have in mind?"

"I think I'd..." Kirsty looked around and saw a display of cat costumes. "I think I'd like to try a cat costume, please," she decided.

"Well we have lots of those in for Halloween," replied Maggie. "How about you, my dear?' she asked Rachel.

Rachel thought fast. They needed to search the shop for the jewel. If Kirsty could keep Maggie busy, then maybe she could look around. "I haven't quite decided yet," she replied truthfully. "Would it be all right if I just have a look first?"

"Of course," Maggie answered. "You go ahead." She smiled at Kirsty. "Now, why don't you come to the changing rooms with me and I'll find a cat costume in your size?"

As Kirsty headed off with Maggie, Rachel glanced round the shop. There were rails of costumes, and shelves piled high with wigs, make-up and masks. Rachel noticed a container full of plastic swords and a stand hung with fairy-like wings and wands. If there is a magic jewel in this shop, she thought, it could be anywhere!

Her eyes fell on a pirate display near the back of the shop. There were two dummies dressed in pirate costumes, each with an eye-patch, standing on a desert island. Between the pirates stood a palm tree and a huge treasure chest, with gold chains and strings of pearls spilling from it. *That would be the perfect place for a jewel to hide,* Rachel thought, hurrying over to the treasure chest.

As she drew closer, her heart seemed to skip a beat. The chest was glowing with a deep golden light. *Magic!* Rachel thought, looking at the way the metal chains glittered and gleamed in the light. It has to be! Holding her breath, she lifted the heavy lid of the chest.

Suddenly, a fountain of orange and gold sparkles shot into the air. Rachel gasped and nearly dropped the lid, for twirling in the middle of the sparkles was a tiny fairy dressed in beautiful, fiery colours!

Costumes Galore!

"Hello!" cried the fairy brightly. She was wearing a yellow skirt with three frills at the bottom, an orange wrap-around top and tiny sparkling orange shoes. Her long, black, wavy hair was held back by a red hairband.

"Hi!" Rachel replied in delight. She thought she recognised the fairy.

"You're Chloe the Topaz Fairy, aren't you?"

Chloe nodded. "That's right."

Rachel glanced over her shoulder. Luckily, Maggie was too busy handing clothes to Kirsty to have noticed anything. Rachel led Chloe behind a costume rail. "Is your Topaz in this shop?" she asked. "Kirsty and I thought there might be a magic jewel in here."

"The magic Topaz is definitely in here. I can feel it," Chloe responded, perching on Rachel's hand. "But I haven't been able to find it. I was searching the treasure chest when the lid fell shut, and I was trapped inside. Thanks for rescuing me."

"That's OK," Rachel declared with a smile. She peeped around the side of the rail. "Have you seen the goblins?"

Chloe looked alarmed. "Goblins! What goblins?"

"There are two in the window pretending to be shop dummies," Rachel explained.

Chloe shivered. "They must be here to guard the Topaz. We'll have to try and send it back to Fairyland without them noticing."

"Yes," Rachel agreed. "But we need to find it first. Where shall we start looking?" Just then she heard the changing-room curtains being pulled back. She peered round the clothes rail to see how her friend was getting on. "That cat costume fits you just fine," Maggie was saying to Kirsty. "But you need some ears. Just wait there while I get you some from the stockroom."

As Maggie moved away, Rachel
hurried over. "Kirsty!" she hissed.

"What is it?" Kirsty
asked eagerly.
"Have you found
something? Oh!"
she gasped, as she
saw Chloe fluttering
beside Rachel.

The little fairy grinned.
"Hi, I'm Chloe," she said.

"Chloe's Topaz is somewhere in here,"
Rachel told Kirsty quietly. "We've got
to find it!"

"What does it look like?" Kirsty asked.

"It's a deep golden colour," Chloe
replied. "And it controls changing
magic, so keep your eyes open for any
strange changes."

"It might be hidden among those fairy wands," Rachel suggested, pointing to a display near the till. "Let's check there."

"You do that while I check the queen costume," Kirsty 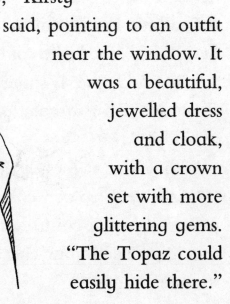 said, pointing to an outfit near the window. It was a beautiful, jewelled dress and cloak, with a crown set with more glittering gems. "The Topaz could easily hide there."

Rachel's sharp ears caught the sound of footsteps. "Maggie's coming back!" she warned, and she and Chloe slipped behind the costume rail again.

"Let's check the fairy display," Rachel whispered to Chloe. "If you hide in the pocket of my coat, Maggie won't see you."

Chloe dived into Rachel's pocket and they headed over to the magic wands.

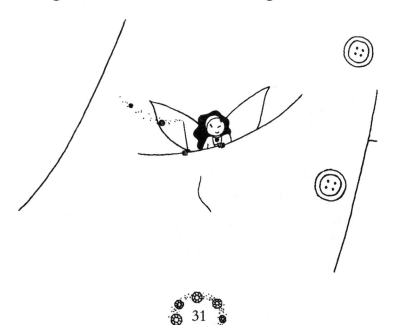

Meanwhile, Maggie was handing the cat ears to Kirsty.

"Um," Kirsty began, "I'm really sorry, but I've just spotted the queen costume, and it's so beautiful! Would you mind if I tried that one on instead?"

"Of course not!" Maggie replied cheerfully. "I'll fetch it for you." She bustled over to the shop window and took the costume off the dummy. "Here we are!" she said, heading back to Kirsty with the costume in her arms.

As Maggie carried the costume past the window, Kirsty heard a faint pop, and saw the air behind Maggie shimmer with a golden glow. Then, to Kirsty's amazement, the witch costume on the goblin in the window changed to a suit of armour! Kirsty gasped and looked around quickly for her friends. She felt certain that the costume change must be the work of Chloe's magic Topaz!

All Change

Maggie drew closer to Kirsty. Behind her, the goblins in the window turned around in confusion. The metal visor on the helmet of the suit of armour fell down with a dull clunk, and the goblin inside let out a muffled shriek of surprise.

Hearing the noise, Maggie swung round. She stared at the suit of armour curiously.

"Where did that come from?" she murmured. "I thought there was a witch costume in the window." She turned back to Kirsty. "Did you see a witch costume?"

Kirsty didn't know what to say. "Um, I can't really remember," she replied.

"Maybe the window dresser changed the costumes yesterday. That was my day off," Maggie explained. "But I'm surprised I didn't notice!"

Behind Maggie, Kirsty could see the
goblin in the red hat
silently sniggering
at his friend, who
was now struggling
to yank open the
heavy visor of his helmet.
Meanwhile, Maggie was shaking out
the queen costume for Kirsty to try on.
As she did so, there was a second faint
pop. Kirsty looked around nervously.

This time she saw the
air shimmer red,
and the bow
and arrows on
a nearby Robin
Hood costume
turned into a
set of bagpipes!

Kirsty's hand flew to her mouth. She hoped Maggie wouldn't notice. She had no idea how she would explain why Robin Hood was clutching the bagpipes! She bit her lip as all the earrings on a display to Maggie's left suddenly turned into pink-and-white stripy sweets. *The Topaz must be in the things that Maggie is holding!* Kirsty thought.

Suddenly, she saw the goblin in armour step cautiously out of the window. He had got his visor open now and his beady eyes were fixed on the robes in Maggie's arms. *Oh no!* Kirsty thought, realising that the goblin must have seen the magic working too.

She watched anxiously as the goblin inched slowly towards Maggie. But, as he did so, one of his big feet knocked into the container of plastic swords.

The rattle made Maggie swing round.

Grabbing a sword, the goblin froze as if he was just another shop display.

"Thanks for the costume," Kirsty said, stepping forward to distract Maggie. "Can I try it on now?"

Throwing the suit of armour a puzzled glance, Maggie turned back to Kirsty. "Of course," she replied, helping Kirsty into the dress and draping the cloak around her shoulders.

As Kirsty took the crown, she noticed a huge golden stone in the centre of it. It seemed to shimmer and shine. Was it the magic Topaz? Kirsty put the crown on, and immediately her head started to tingle with fairy magic. "Oh, wow!" she breathed.

"Do you like it?" Maggie smiled.
"I think I've got a sceptre in the
stockroom that would look lovely with
that costume. I'll see if I can find it
for you."

As soon as Maggie had gone, Kirsty
turned to Rachel and Chloe who were
at the fairy display. "I've got the
Topaz!" she called softly.

"Hooray!" Rachel
exclaimed.

"Where is it?"
asked Chloe,
zooming out
of Rachel's
pocket in a
whoosh of sparks.

"In the crown on
my head!" replied Kirsty.

Rachel looked at Kirsty's head in surprise. "Crown?" she asked. "Do you mean the turban?"

Curiously, Kirsty turned to look in the changing-room mirror. Immediately, she saw that the crown had changed into a turban, but the golden Topaz still glittered at its centre. "It's changed!" she breathed.

At that moment, Rachel let out a cry of alarm. "Kirsty!"

"Watch out!" Chloe exclaimed at the same time.

Kirsty whirled round to see that the goblin in armour had crept up on her while she wasn't looking. Now, cackling gleefully, he gave a great leap and snatched the turban and the Topaz right off Kirsty's head!

Stop that Goblin!

"I've got the Topaz!" the goblin shouted, staggering down the shop with the turban and its precious, glowing jewel.

"After him!" Kirsty cried, as the goblin charged towards the shop door, his metal armour clanking.

Rachel and Chloe raced after him.

"Come on!" the goblin in the red hat shouted, running up the steps towards the door. But the armour wasn't easy for his friend to run in. The visor fell down over his eyes again and, unable to see anything, he bumped clumsily into the pile of Halloween lanterns, sending them bouncing and rolling across the floor.

The goblin tripped over one of them and lost his balance. "Whaaaa!" he cried, tumbling onto his back among the pumpkins. As he fell, the turban slipped from his grasp and flew through the air.

"You slug-brained idiot!" the other goblin spluttered. "What do you think you are doing?"

"I can't see," the armoured goblin whined, trying to tug his visor up. "And now I've hurt my bottom!"

"Catch that turban, Rachel!" Kirsty exclaimed, as the turban plummeted towards the ground.

Rachel reached for it, but missed. As the turban hit the ground, the Topaz was jolted out of its setting. Bouncing across the floor, the golden gem rolled straight in amongst the scattered pumpkins. There was a loud pop, a shimmer of golden light and, in the blink of an eye, all the pumpkins had changed into pineapples!

"Where's the Topaz?" Kirsty cried, lifting the hem of her costume and running over.

"I can see it!" Chloe gasped, swooping towards the pineapples and pointing with her wand.

Kirsty saw the Topaz glowing amongst the fruit. But as Chloe zoomed towards it, the goblin by the door saw it too. Sliding through the pineapples as if he was on ice, he scooped the Topaz up with one hand just before Chloe reached it.

"Ow!" he wailed as the heat of the magic jewel burnt his icy goblin skin.

For a moment, Kirsty felt a burst of hope. She remembered that goblins couldn't touch the magic jewels with their bare hands without getting burnt. She waited for the goblin to drop the Topaz.

But instead there was another loud pop, and the goblin's tunic and hat changed into a teddy-bear costume, complete with furry gloves that looked like paws!

"I've got the Topaz!" the teddy-bear goblin shouted triumphantly to his friend, who was scrambling out of his metal armour. "Let's get out of here!" Clutching the jewel in his furry paws, he charged back towards the door.

Chloe swooped at the teddy-bear goblin's head. "Give me my jewel!" she cried.

"Shan't!" he shouted rudely. "The Topaz isn't yours anymore. It's ours, and you're never going to get it back!"

"Come on, Kirsty!" Rachel cried. "We've got to stop them!"

She and Kirsty began to run through the pineapples, trying not to trip on the fruit. The goblins had reached the steps. Rachel was horrified to see that they were going to get away with the Topaz. But then, suddenly, she had an idea. She picked up

a pineapple as if it was a bowling ball, and then, with a thrust of her arm, she sent it whizzing along the floor – straight at the two goblins.

The pineapple hit the feet of the goblin who had been in armour. He cried out in surprise and grabbed the arm of the teddy-bear goblin who was halfway up the steps. For a moment, both goblins teetered on the steps, arms flailing, and then they toppled down the stairs to land in a heap.

The Topaz was flung from the
goblin's furry paw and went
spinning through the air.
As it flew past the
lights there was
a pop, the air
shimmered with
an amber glow
and suddenly all
the shop lights
became tiny
round disco balls
that dazzled and
shone with magic.

Chloe plunged after the
jewel, and caught it in both
hands. But it was too heavy for
her to fly with. "Whoa!" she cried in
alarm, her wings fluttering frantically.

She and the jewel sank towards
the ground. "Help!"
Seeing what was
happening, Kirsty
scrambled to her feet
and dived towards
the fairy with her
hands outstretched.
The fairy and the
Topaz landed
safely in her palms.
Kirsty pulled her
hands to her chest,
her heart beating fast.
Was Chloe OK?
"Phew!" Chloe said,
poking her head out of
Kirsty's cupped hands and grinning.
"Thanks for catching me, Kirsty!"

"Are you all right?" Rachel asked, scrambling over and looking at her in concern.

"I'm fine," Chloe replied. Her hair was standing on end, but her brown eyes were sparkling. "In fact, I'm better than fine," she said, looking at the groaning goblins, "now that I've got my Topaz back!"

Just then, there was a noise from the stockroom. "I've found the sceptre!" came Maggie's cheerful voice. "I'll be out in a minute, once I've put these boxes away."

"Oh, no!" Rachel gasped in horror. "I'd forgotten about Maggie."

She looked around at the shop. There were pineapples all over the floor, glittering mirror balls instead of lights, and bits of armour scattered everywhere – not to mention the fact that the window display was ruined because its two main stars were in a heap by the door!

"Maggie will be horrified by all this mess!" Kirsty said.

"Don't worry," Chloe replied cheerfully. "Now I've got the Topaz back, I can work some changing magic." She touched her golden wand to the Topaz in Kirsty's hand.

The tip of the wand began to gleam like a ray of sparkling sunshine. Lifting it high in the air, the little fairy waved it expertly.

There was a quick series of pops, like popcorn bursting in a pan, and everything started to change again. The air glimmered orange, then red, and finally gold, as the pineapples changed back to pumpkins, the disco lights changed to normal lights, two proper shop dummies appeared in the window and everything was magically back the way it had been in the first place. Even the bits of armour were neatly on a shelf. With a final loud pop, all the bits of armour jumped neatly onto a shelf.

"Phew!" Rachel said in relief.

Chloe smiled at her. "It's all back to normal."

"Except for one thing," Kirsty said slowly, looking at the door. "What's Maggie going to say when she sees those goblins?"

Fluffy Bunnies

The goblins were picking themselves up off the floor, groaning and arguing. Their costumes had disappeared and they were back to their ordinary, green goblin selves.

"Why did you trip me up like that?" the first goblin demanded.

"Why did you let the Topaz go?"

spluttered the other. "Butterfingers!"

"Don't call me butterfingers!" the
first goblin shouted.

"Oh, dear, I think those two are
going to take some explaining,"
Rachel said.

"Leave it to me!" Chloe flew over
to the goblins.
"Pesky fairy!"
snarled the first
goblin, making a
swipe at Chloe,
who darted easily
out of his way. "Give
us the Topaz back!"

"No," Chloe replied
coolly. "And my wand is charged
up with changing magic now, so
I can turn you into anything I like!"

She smiled. "And if you don't leave the shop this minute, I'm going to turn you both into fluffy, pink bunny rabbits!"

The goblins' mouths dropped open in horror.

"Bunny rabbits!" the first one exclaimed. "Yuck!"

"You wouldn't!" said the second.

Chloe grinned. "Oh yes I would." She shot a look at Rachel and Kirsty.

"What do you two think?"

Rachel grinned back. "I think they'd make lovely bunny rabbits," she said.

"Especially fluffy pink ones," Kirsty added.

Chloe lifted her wand.

"Noooooo!" both goblins cried in alarm, and they turned and ran up the steps. Fighting each other out of the way, they yanked the shop door open and disappeared down the high street at top speed.

Rachel, Kirsty and Chloe
burst out laughing.

"You girls seem
to be having a
good time,"
Maggie said,
emerging from
the stockroom with
a sceptre in her hand.

Chloe darted into Rachel's
pocket just in time.

"I'm sorry I was so long." Maggie added,
looking at the door which was swinging
open. "Have I missed a customer?"

"It's OK," said Kirsty, quickly putting
the Topaz back in her pocket. "It was
just, er..."

"Someone looking for pineapples,"
Rachel finished quickly.

Kirsty hid a grin as Maggie looked at Rachel in surprise. "Pineapples?" she queried.

Rachel nodded. "When they realised you didn't sell any, they left," she added.

"Oh, right." Maggie blinked. "Well, never mind. Here's the sceptre," she said, handing it to Kirsty. She turned to Rachel. "Have you decided on your costume yet?"

"I think I'd like to go as a fairy,"
Rachel replied. "You've got some
lovely fairy wings and wands."

"Yes," Kirsty agreed, handing the
sceptre back carefully. "Thank you for
letting me try the costumes on,
but I think I'd like to go
as a fairy too." She saw
Chloe's head pop out
of Rachel's pocket.
The fairy grinned
and gave her a
thumbs-up sign
before quickly
ducking down so
Maggie wouldn't see her.

Kirsty changed out of the Queen's
costume and the girls chose a pair of
wings and a wand each. Just as they

Chloe

finished paying for them the phone rang. "Enjoy your Halloween party, girls," Maggie said as she hurried off to answer the call.

The moment she was gone, Chloe  flew out of Rachel's pocket in a cloud of fairy dust. "I wish I could stay and see you off to your party. I bet you'll look great in your fairy costumes, but I'd better get back to Fairyland now. Thank you for helping me rescue the Topaz." Kirsty took the stone out of her pocket. "Here it is," she said, holding it out.

68

Chloe touched her wand to the golden jewel, and in a fountain of orange sparkles it disappeared safely back to Fairyland.

Rachel and Kirsty picked up their shopping bags containing their wings and wands and headed out of the shop.

"See you soon!" Chloe said as Rachel pulled the door open.

"Bye," the girls called as the little fairy spun round in a swirl of golden light and then zoomed away.

"I'm glad we were able to help her," Rachel said happily.

"Me too," Kirsty agreed. A sparkle near the ceiling caught her eye, and she looked up curiously. A single tiny disco ball was still hanging there, glittering and shining with fairy magic. "Look!" she exclaimed. "Chloe left one little mirror ball behind."

Rachel laughed. "There'll always be magic in the shop now," she said. Then she spotted the bus turning into the high street. "Come on!" she gasped, pulling the door shut behind them. "We've got to catch the bus, Kirsty!"

They began to run down the street. "It's been an amazing day, hasn't it?" Kirsty panted. "What do you think will happen tomorrow?"

"I don't know," Rachel said, as they reached the bus stop just in time and jumped on board. She grinned at Kirsty. "But it's bound to be something magic!"

RAINBOW magic ®

The Jewel Fairies

India, Scarlett, Emily and Chloe have
got their jewels back. Now Rachel
and Kirsty must help

Amy the Amethyst Fairy

Win a Rainbow Magic
Sparkly T-Shirt and Goody Bag!

In every book in the Rainbow Magic Jewel Fairies
series (books 22-28) there is a hidden picture of a jewel with
a secret letter in it. Find all seven letters and
re-arrange them to make a special Fairyland word,
then send it to us. Each month we will put the entries into a
draw and select one winner to receive a
Rainbow Magic Sparkly T-shirt and Goody Bag!

Send your entry on a postcard to Rainbow Magic Jewel
Competition, Orchard Books, 96 Leonard Street,
London EC2A 4XD. Australian readers should
write to Hachette Children's Books, Level 17/207
Kent Street, Sydney, NSW 2000.
Don't forget to include your name and address.
Only one entry per child. Final draw: 30th September 2006.

Coming Soon...
Stella the Star Fairy

STELLA THE STAR FAIRY

1-84362-869-4

Stella the Star Fairy can't keep Christmas
bright and shiny without her three magical
tree decorations. Can Kirsty and Rachel
help her get them back to the fairy tree
by Christmas Eve, or will the season
be ruined for everyone?

by Daisy Meadows